Shout Daisy SHOUT!

Jane Simmons

ORCHARD BOOKS

To Ruby and Denis who never shout

Other great Daisy books

Come On, Daisy!

Daisy and the Egg

Daisy and the Beastie

- picture books and chunky board books

Daisy's Hide and Seek

- lift the flap board book

Bouncy Bouncy Daisy

Splish Splash Daisy

- first jigsaw books

ORCHARD BOOKS
96 Leonard Street, London EC2A 4XD
Orchard Books Australia
32/45-51 Huntley Street, Alexandria, NSW 2015
ISBN 1 84121 547 3 (hardback)
ISBN 1 84121 268 7 (paperback)
First published in Great Britain in 2002
First paperback publication in 2003
Copyright © Jane Simmons 2002
The right of Jane Simmons to be identified as the author and illustrator
of this work has been asserted by her in accordance with the
Copyright, Designs and Patents Act, 1988.
A CIP catalogue record for this book is available from the British Library.
3 5 7 9 10 8 6 4 2 (hardback)
3 5 7 9 10 8 6 4 2 (paperback)
Printed in Singapore

Daisy loved visiting Auntie Lily's, there was always so much to play with.

There were the flowers.
"Buzz!" buzzed Daisy,
"Buzz!" squeaked Pip,
but the bees flew away.

And there was the bird table.
"Tweet!" squawked Daisy,
"Squeak!" squeaked Pip, but
the birds took off too.
"Oh dear," said Auntie Lily.
"Try being a bit quieter," said Mamma Duck

Daisy tried, but she wasn't quiet for long.

eek

eek

. . . and the mice ran away.

splish

splosh

. . . and the
fish went too.

And even the balloon
floated up, up and away.

Then there was nothing
left to play with.

"Come on," said Auntie Lily,
"I know a perfect place for
being noisy!" and they all set off.

Everyone was quacking so loudly.
"Now you can make as much
noise as you like!" said Auntie Lily.

QUACK

QUACK

QUACK

QUACK

QUACK

QUACK

QUACK

QUACK

quack

quack

quack

quack

quack

quack quack quack

QUACK

QUACK

QUACK

Then the bread came out and everyone dived for it.
"Shout Daisy SHOUT!" Auntie Lily called out.
"QUACK!" shouted Daisy at the top of her voice.
"QUACK!" squeaked Pip as they raced for a bit.

They got it,

and pulled

and pulled.

It broke in two.

They softened it

and munched
it down.

QUACK
QUACK
QUACK
QUACK
QUACK
QUACK
QUACK
QUACK
QUACK
quack
quack

Suddenly there were ducks everywhere, everyone was quacking! "Daisy! Pip!" shouted Mamma.

Daisy couldn't see Mamma
or Auntie Lily anywhere.
"Where's Mamma?" cried Pip.

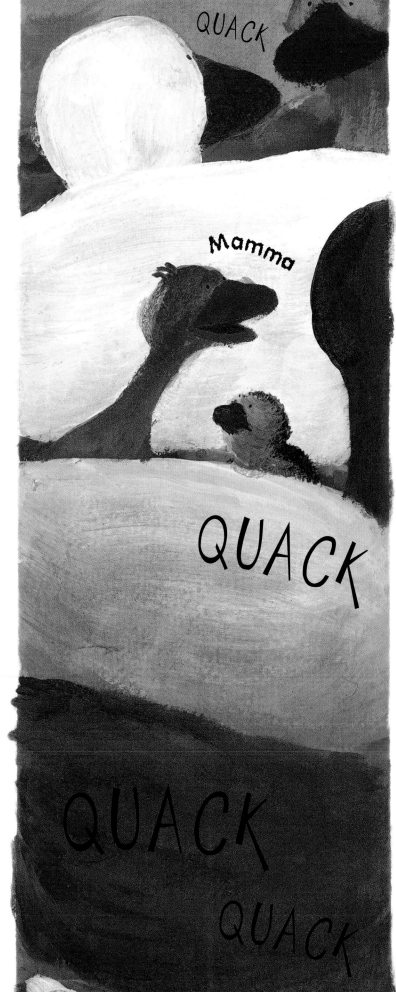

But all the quacking was too loud.

"Mamma!" cried Pip.
"She can't hear us," said Daisy.

QUACK

QUACK

More bread
came and
everyone was
pushing and
shoving and shouting.

QUACK

QUACK

QUACK

"Shout Daisy
SHOUT!" cried Pip.
Daisy took the
deepest breath ever . . .

Everything went quiet.

And there through the crowd was
Mamma Duck and Auntie Lily.
"What a voice!" said Auntie Lily.
"Oh yes," said Mamma Duck proudly.
"Mamma!" cried Pip and Daisy, and
off they went, back to Auntie Lily's . . . .

. . . for a very, very quiet afternoon.